W9-AAK-473

Edited by Anna McQuinn and Ambreen Husain
Designed by Suzy McGrath and Sarah Godwin

First published in the United States in 1996 by
De Agostini Editions Ltd, 919 Third Avenue,
New York, NY 10022

Distributed by Stewart, Tabori & Chang
a division of U.S. Media Holdings, Inc.,
New York, NY

ISBN 1-899883-60-6
Library of Congress Catalog Card
Number: 96-83070

Printed and bound in Italy

Food Science Consultant
Shirley Corriher

For Faye, CF
For my own Magic Mom, HR

My Mom is MAGIC!

Written by

Hannah Roche

Illustrated by

Chris Fisher

My mom is magic!

Today she took out two eggs.

She separated
the yellow yolk
from the clear,
gooey part.

She put the gooey stuff in a bowl
and whisked really hard.

It got bigger and bigger
and fluffier and fluffier!

And then, guess what she did...

she turned the bowl right upside down
...and it didn't fall out!

My mom is magic!

Next, Mom added sugar.

Then I put spoonfuls of
the fluffy mixture on
the baking sheet, and
Mom put it in the oven.

They were there for a really long
time – I kept checking!

Mom told me
to be patient,
and not touch
the hot oven.

Then – **Abracadabra**
they'd turned into
meringues!

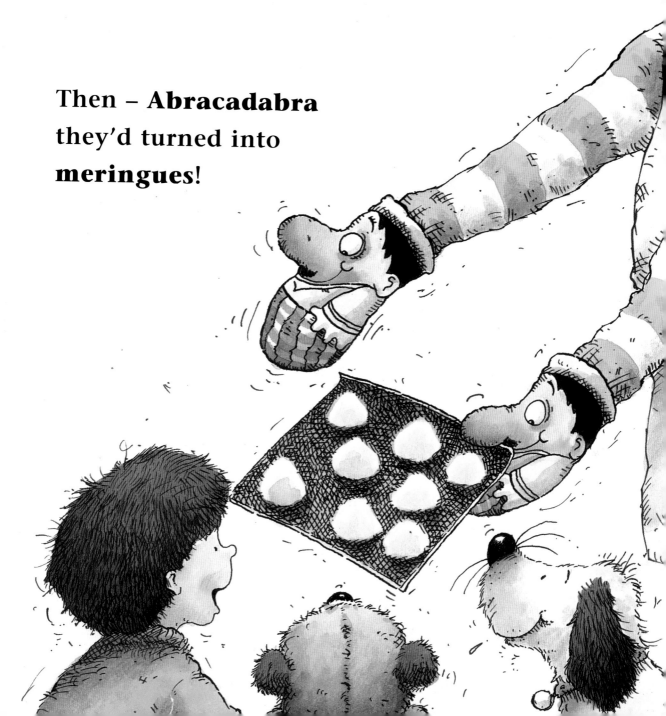

They are hard on the outside,
sticky in the middle and
yummy and sugary.

I love my magic mom!

Notes for Parents

EVEN very young children are aware that water is wet, rock is hard, sand is grainy. As they observe more, children discover that things don't always stay the same – whipping, heating, mixing, freezing and so on make things change from watery to fluffy, from soft to hard, from liquid to solid....

LEARNING to notice and describe the textures and changes is important to children's understanding of the world around them. Don't worry about using "proper" scientific words – getting the description right is what really matters.

YOU can recreate the story in your own kitchen by following the recipe opposite. As you go along, encourage your child to talk about what's happening. Then, you can eat the results!

HOW IT WORKS

WHEN you whip egg whites, the egg white proteins unwind and expand, forming elastic-walled cells that trap air. The air is what makes the egg whites fluffy.

BEATEN EGG WHITES stick to the bottom of the bowl due to surface tension. Surface tension is what holds drops of water together in "beads" on shiny surfaces like kitchen counters.

Jamie's Recipe

YOU WILL NEED:

2 eggs
half a cup of sugar
a bowl, a tablespoon
a baking sheet
a whisk or electric mixer
parchment paper

1. Preheat your oven to 275°F.
2. Line a baking sheet with parchment paper.
3. Separate the egg whites from the yolks.
4. Whisk the whites until stiff, when you can turn the bowl upside down.
5. Then whisk in half of the sugar, a little at a time.
6. When this mixture is really stiff, carefully fold in the remaining sugar.
7. Spoon the mixture in heaped tablespoon amounts onto the baking sheet.
8. Place in the oven for about an hour or until completely dry.
9. Serve the meringues on their own, or with fruit and cream or ice cream.

HINTS

CHILDREN can easily separate egg whites by carefully breaking the egg into a saucer, covering the yolk completely with a narrow juice glass, then draining the white into a bowl.

DO NOT allow any yolk to escape as yolk contains fat which makes the eggs difficult to whip. A metal bowl will also help.

MAKE sure the eggs are at room temperature, not straight from the fridge.